KIDS' SPORT STORIES

BASKETBALL
CAMP GO-GETTER

by Dionna L. Mann

illustrated by Amanda Erb

raintree

a Capstone company — publishers for children

Raintree is an imprint of Capstone Global Library Limited, a company
incorporated in England and Wales having its registered office at 264
Banbury Road, Oxford, OX2 7DY – Registered company number:
6695582

www.raintree.co.uk
myorders@raintree.co.uk

Edited by Carrie Sheely
Designed by Bobbie Nuytten
Original illustrations © Capstone Global Library Limited 2023
Picture research by Morgan Walters
Production by Polly Fisher
Originated by Capstone Global Library Ltd

978 1 3982 4824 3

British Library Cataloguing in Publication Data
A full catalogue record for this book is available from the British Library.

Printed and bound in India.

CONTENTS

Glossary

 **basket** net that is connected to the metal ring on a basketball hoop; when the ball goes through the basket at least one point is scored

 **dribble** bounce a basketball off the floor using one hand

 **pivot** turn around quickly

 **push rim** metal outer part of a wheel on a wheelchair that is used to push the wheelchair forward

 **swish** when the ball goes into the basket without hitting the rim or backboard; the ball makes a swishing sound as it goes through the net

Chapter 1
READY TO PLAY

Zoe waved goodbye to her mum. She had just arrived at the first day of basketball camp. She knew it would be fun, even though she'd never played basketball before.

Inside the gym, Zoe saw some kids about her age. One girl smiled at Zoe. Zoe smiled back, then rolled over to the sign-in table.

"Welcome to basketball camp!" a teen girl said. She got Zoe signed in and told her what they'd be learning at camp. "You can head over to Coach Mike at the other side of the gym. He'll get you a sport wheelchair," she said.

Zoe was excited to try new moves with a sport wheelchair.

"Happy you've joined us, Zoe!" Coach Mike said. He helped Zoe get comfortable in the chair. "You can go over to the court. We'll get started soon."

As Zoe started moving, the new chair's large **push rims** felt great in her hands.

The girl who had smiled at Zoe came over. "Hi, my name is Brooklyn. Is this your first time at camp?" Brooklyn asked.

"Yes," said Zoe. "I really want to learn to play."

Just then, Pax and Vinny rolled over.

"Hi, guys," Brooklyn said. "This is Zoe."

"Hi, Zoe! Check this out!" Pax said as he twirled a basketball on his finger.

"That's nothing," Vinny said. "Watch this!" Vinny did a quick spin in his wheelchair.

Zoe laughed. Basketball was going to be great!

Chapter 2
ONE GOAL SHORT

That night, Zoe made a goal for each week of camp. *I am going to be a great player by the end of camp,* thought Zoe.

For week one of camp, Zoe wanted to be able to use her sports wheelchair like a pro. By the week's end, Zoe had met her goal! She could **pivot**, spin circles and make figure eights.

For week two, Zoe had a new goal –
dribbling well.

Brooklyn offered to help Zoe. "This is
how I do it," she said.

Brooklyn placed the ball on her lap,
then pushed her chair hard two times.
While coasting, she dribbled the ball with
one hand.

Brooklyn passed the ball to Zoe. "Give it
a try!" she said.

Zoe put the ball on her lap. Push one, push two! She dropped the ball. Bounce! She was off!

"You're a natural!" Brooklyn said, smiling.

By the week's end, Zoe had met her second goal.

For her next goal, Zoe wanted to get the ball in the **basket**. But whenever she tried, the ball fell short.

Pax said, "Try pointing your hand like this. Pretend it's an arrow telling your ball where to go."

Pax aimed. **Swish!** The ball dropped through the basket.

Zoe dribbled towards the basket. She aimed like Pax. The ball missed. Zoe frowned.

Brooklyn said, "Give it time."

Pax rolled over. "Your aim looks better! The baskets will come with practice," he said.

But the last day of camp was just two days away. Zoe didn't have time.

Chapter 3
SWISH!

The next day, Zoe wanted to practise shooting. But Coach got them to work on passing. When they finally started shooting, not one of Zoe's shots made it in the basket.

How would she ever meet her final goal?
Zoe was frustrated. When a ball rolled
towards her, she threw it – hard.

Coach Mike came over. "Zoe, what's wrong?"

"I thought I'd be able to make shots by now," Zoe said.

"Be patient. You'll get there," Coach said.

Zoe was not feeling patient.

On the last day of camp, Zoe rolled slowly into the gym for the final game. Brooklyn, Pax and Vinny greeted her.

"We're going to help you make a basket," Brooklyn said.

"Watch out, world," Vinny said, "Star scorer coming up!"

"Let's go!" Pax said.

As the game started, Zoe's friends kept passing her the ball. Zoe had plenty of chances to score. Still, the first half ended without her scoring. During the break, Zoe felt like crying.

"You passed perfectly," said Brooklyn.

"You caught like a pro," said Pax.

"Your dribbling was outstanding," said Vinny.

Zoe thought about it. Maybe she should shift her focus.

After half-time, Zoe stopped thinking about making a shot. She focused on passing and dribbling. She cheered when her friends scored.

As the game was winding down, Zoe caught the ball. She dribbled towards the basket. She aimed. The ball flew and . . . Swish! Zoe scored!

Everyone cheered.

Zoe felt very proud.

"See you next year?" Brooklyn asked Zoe as they were saying goodbye.

"That's the goal!" Zoe said. They both laughed.

EGG CATCH

In wheelchair basketball, coaches sometimes get players to play catch with an egg. The game helps them practise their passing and catching skills. Give it a try with your friends and see who wins!

What you need:
- a chair for each person
- an egg for each pair

What to do:
- Sit outside in chairs opposite one another. Start about 1.5 metres (5 feet) apart.
- Take turns throwing the egg with your partner. Aim the egg at your partner's hand. As you catch, gently move your hand back to help absorb the force of the pass.
- After a few successful passes, increase the distance between your chairs. Some wheelchair basketball players can pass and catch eggs while sitting 15 metres (50 feet) apart! There's a goal for you!

  Tip: You can try using water balloons instead of eggs.

Take another look at this illustration. Zoe was frustrated because she wasn't able to meet her last goal fast enough. Have you ever been frustrated while learning something new? What do you think Zoe could have done differently to stop herself getting frustrated?

Write down a big goal you have. Then break it down into smaller goals, and write them down. Then get going on completing them, and stay positive!

ABOUT THE AUTHOR

Dionna L. Mann is a children's book author and freelance journalist who in her younger days loved biking, swimming, jogging and meandering through the woods. She spent more than 25 years volunteering and working in the school system where her talented now-grown children attended. Her favourite part of working with children was teaching them about the writing process and reading the beautiful and heartfelt words they penned. As a person of colour, she enjoys learning about lesser-known people found in the records of African American history. One day she hopes to swim with dolphins.

ABOUT
THE ILLUSTRATOR

Amanda Erb is an illustrator from Massachusetts, USA. She earned a BFA in illustration from Ringling College of Art and Design. In her free time, she enjoys playing football, learning Spanish and discovering new stories to read.